Nina
the Birthday Cake Fairy

For magical Myla Ramsden

Special thanks to Rachel Elliot

ISBN 978-0-545-60537-3

12 11 10 9 8 7 6 5 4 3 2 1   14 15 16 17 18 19/0

Printed in China   68

This edition first printing, March 2014

Nina
the Birthday Cake Fairy

by Daisy Meadows

SCHOLASTIC INC.

The Fairyland Palace

Candy Land

Goblins' ice cream truck

Market booth

Charlie's ice cream truck

Kirsty's House

Wetherbury Village

Jack Frost's
Ice Castle

Fair

The Park

Candy
Shop

High St.

I have a plan to make a mess
And cause the fairies much distress.
I'm going to take their charms away
And make my dreams come true today!

I'll build a castle made of sweets,
And ruin the fairies' silly treats.
I just don't care how much they whine,
Their cakes and candies will be mine!

Contents

Cake Calamity

"What an amazing birthday this has been!" said Kirsty Tate, twirling happily in the middle of the sidewalk.

"It's been the most fun birthday ever," agreed her best friend, Rachel Walker. "I've enjoyed it just as much as you, even though it's not even MY birthday!"

1

Rachel was visiting the Tate family for spring break. Right now, they were walking home from Wetherbury Park with Kirsty's parents. They had been celebrating Kirsty's birthday at the village fair!

"So, what's been the best thing about your birthday so far?" asked Mr. Tate.

Kirsty threw her hands into the air. "I can't decide!" she said with a laugh. "Everything has been perfect. Rachel's here,

Aunt Helen gave us a tour of Candy Land, and we had a great time at the fair."

"Well, your birthday is about to get even better," said Mrs. Tate, raising an eyebrow.

Kirsty stopped and looked at her parents and Rachel. Their eyes were all sparkling with happiness.

"We have another birthday surprise for you," Mr. Tate added.

Kirsty looked at their smiling faces in excitement. What could it be?

"You have to tell me what the surprise is!" she pleaded.

Rachel shook her head. "That would ruin it," she said. "Come on, let's hurry back to your house."

The girls held hands and rushed ahead.

"It's really hard to keep secrets from you," Rachel said breathlessly. "We usually share everything!"

In fact, the girls shared one of the biggest secrets imaginable. They were friends with the fairies! Their latest magical adventures were some of the most thrilling they'd ever had.

"My birthday would be absolutely

perfect if we could just help the last Sugar and Spice Fairy get her charm back from Jack Frost," said Kirsty.

Two days ago, Jack Frost and his goblins had stolen the magic charms that belonged to the seven Sugar and Spice Fairies. Honey the Candy Fairy had come to ask the girls for their help.

"We've already found six of the magic charms," said Rachel proudly. "There's just one more to find."

The Sugar and Spice Fairies needed their charms to create all kinds of delicious sweet treats in Fairyland and the human world. But Jack Frost wanted all the treats for his own special project—a giant Candy Castle! He gave the Sugar and Spice Fairies' charms to his goblins for safekeeping, and ordered

them to bring back all the yummy treats from the human world.

"The worst part is that today is Treat Day in Fairyland," said Kirsty. "If Queen Titania and King Oberon don't have goodies to put in the fairies' treat baskets, Treat Day will have to be canceled!"

At that moment, they reached Kirsty's front door. Rachel gave her best friend's hand a squeeze.

"Forget about Jack Frost for now," she said. "We can think about how to find the last charm later. Right now, your last birthday treat is waiting!"

Kirsty's parents caught up to them and opened the door. As Kirsty stepped inside, there was a loud shout.

"SURPRISE!"

Aunt Helen and all of Kirsty's friends from school jumped out, waving balloons and tossing confetti! Kirsty's mouth fell open and her eyes grew wide.

"A party?" she said in an amazed whisper. "I can't believe it. I had no idea!"

Everyone laughed and cheered, and then her friends pulled her into the living room. It was beautifully decorated with pink, yellow, and turquoise balloons, rainbow-colored flags, and a big HAPPY BIRTHDAY, KIRSTY banner.

"This is fantastic," said Kirsty. "Thank you all so much!"

"Happy birthday!" said Rachel, giving her best friend a big hug.

"Come into the kitchen and see your cake," said Aunt Helen, her eyes shining.

She led the girls into the kitchen, where they saw a large box sitting on the counter. It was a cake box from the best bakery in the village, Cupcake Corner. Kirsty clapped her hands together in delight.

"I love Cupcake Corner!" she exclaimed.

Aunt Helen grinned at her.

"Then you're in for a treat," she said. "Ta-da!"

She flung open the box—and then gasped with dismay. Instead of a beautiful cake, there were only a few crumbs inside!

A Surprise in the Shed

"I can't figure out where the cake could have gone," said Aunt Helen, frowning. "Maybe someone took it to put candles on top. I'll go and check."

She hurried out of the kitchen. Just then, they heard Kirsty's friend Myla in the living room.

"Musical chairs!" she called. "Come on, everyone!"

Soon, Kirsty and Rachel were alone in the kitchen. They exchanged a worried look.

"This must be the work of Jack Frost and his goblins," said Rachel.

As the music started up in the next room, Kirsty leaned over and examined the cake box.

"I wonder if they left any clues," she said.

Just then, the musical chairs music stopped. In the silence, the girls heard a soft sob.

"That sounded like a fairy!" said Rachel in an excited whisper.

"That glob of icing is glowing," said Kirsty, pointing to a corner of the box.

To their delight, a tiny fairy peeked out from behind the icing!

"It's Nina the Birthday Cake Fairy," exclaimed Rachel. "Hello, Nina!"

But Nina could hardly speak. Sparkly fairy tears ran down her face.

"Oh, girls," she said, sniffing. "I feel so helpless!  I just saw Jack Frost steal your birthday cake, Kirsty, and I couldn't stop him. He has my magic birthday candle charm! I'm so sorry."

13

The girls couldn't stand to see Nina so upset. They wished that they were fairy-size so that they could put their arms around her. She needed a hug!

"Please don't cry," said Kirsty. "We'll help you get your charm back."

"Hey, look!" said Rachel, pointing. "There are some crumbs outside the box, too."

"It looks like a trail," said Kirsty. "Come on—we might be able to catch up with Jack Frost!"

At once, Nina brushed her tears away. She zoomed into the air, looking very determined. She hid in the pocket of Kirsty's skirt, and the girls glanced at each other. In the living

room, the music had started up again.

"No one will miss us yet," said
Rachel. "They're all enjoying the
party. Hopefully we can get back
before they realize we're gone!"

The trail of crumbs led out the back
door and across the yard. Rachel and
Kirsty ran lightly across the grass,
following the delicious-looking crumbs
until they reached the shed.

"Look, the door's half open," whispered Kirsty. "Mom and Dad always close it. There must be someone inside!"

They poked their heads around the door. Inside, someone was standing with his back to them. He was wearing an ice-blue cape, and his hair was very spiky.

"Jack Frost!" said Kirsty under her breath.

"And look what's next to him," Rachel whispered.

On an upturned crate was a glittering, pink birthday cake. On the top, in rose-colored icing, were the words HAPPY BIRTHDAY, KIRSTY.

Jack Frost rubbed his hands together and cackled with laughter.

"It can be my birthday every day now that I have Nina's magic charm," he gloated. "I'm going to have the biggest birthday party EVER at my Candy Castle, with lots of presents and birthday songs. I'll have ALL the treats from Fairyland and the human world. Best of all, I'll have mountains of birthday cake! It serves those pesky fairies right!"

He raised his wand and zapped the birthday cake with a blast of icy magic. The rose-colored icing seemed to dribble and run. Soon, it was replaced with ice-blue writing that said HAPPY BIRTHDAY, JACK FROST.

Rachel couldn't bear to watch anymore! She felt angry and upset for her best friend. She pushed the shed door open and marched inside. Her eyes were blazing.

"Stop that cackling right now," she demanded. "Give Kirsty's birthday cake back. You're ruining her birthday!"

"Give Nina's magic charm back, too," added Kirsty, hurrying into the shed after Rachel. "You have to stop being so mean and selfish. Otherwise, birthday cakes *everywhere* will be ruined."

"I don't care!" shouted Jack Frost. He cackled again and hurled a bolt of magic at them. The girls dove out of the way, and heard a loud *bang*, followed by a puff of blue smoke. When the

smoke cleared, Jack Frost had
disappeared. And so had the birthday
cake!

Nina fluttered up out of Kirsty's pocket
and waved her
wand. The girls
were instantly
caught up in
a candy-
colored swirl
of fairy dust!
They felt
themselves
shrinking to
fairy-size. They
wiggled their shoulders happily as fairy
wings appeared on their backs. When
the fairy dust cleared, they found

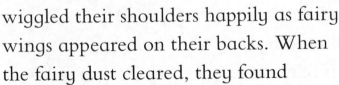

themselves hovering high above
Fairyland.

"It's wonderful to be back here!" said
Rachel, doing a somersault in the air.

"I love being a fairy," added Kirsty
with a laugh, shaking a few colorful
specks of fairy dust from her hair.

"There's Jack Frost's Candy Castle,"
said Nina, pointing down at the cupcake
turrets and the doors made of cookies.
"Girls, this could be dangerous. Are you
sure you want to come with me?"

"Of course!" said Rachel, sounding
brave. "We're not letting Jack Frost ruin
Treat Day—or Kirsty's birthday!"

Jack Frost's Birthday

The girls and Nina flew toward the castle as fast as their wings would take them. They landed on the branch of a chocolate tree and looked up. The castle loomed high above them, rising out of the milkshake moat that surrounded the grounds.

"That's funny," said Rachel. "Even though the castle is brand-new, it looks like it's crumbling."

"Maybe those goblin builders are here to repair it," said Kirsty.

She pointed to dozens of goblins who were lingering around the castle. They were all dressed in green overalls and green hard hats, and they were standing very close to the walls.

"They're not building it," said Kirsty with a gasp. "They're EATING it!"

She was right. The troublesome goblins were sneaking bites of the Candy Castle!

"There were goblins eating the castle yesterday, too," Rachel said. "Remember, Kirsty? We saw them when we came here with Clara the Chocolate Fairy."

"Yes," said Kirsty. "Wow, it looks terrible! It's covered in bite-shaped holes."

Nina gave a sudden, sharp gasp.

"Look down, girls!" she whispered.

Below them, a long-nosed goblin was nibbling on the trunk of the chocolate tree. He had pieces of chocolate bark in each hand, and chocolate-milk sap was running down his chin.

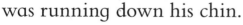

"Jack Frost's Candy Castle will disappear in days if the greedy goblins keep doing this," said Rachel.

Just then, they heard a bell ringing. The gates of the Candy Castle opened, and out came a goblin dressed as an old-fashioned town crier. He was wearing a black three-cornered hat topped with a white feather, a long red-and-gold cape, cropped black pants, and a pair of white tights. He was even carrying a large bell. The other goblins all stopped eating the castle and stared at him. Then they started giggling and pointing.

The town-crier goblin stuck his tongue out at them and rang his bell again.

"Hear ye, hear ye!" he bellowed. "Today is Jack Frost's birthday. Every goblin is ordered to come to the tent in the garden to sing 'Happy Birthday.' Presents are required, and any goblin who doesn't come will be in BIG TROUBLE. There will be birthday cake!"

As soon as they heard the word *cake*, the other goblins stopped giggling. They all raced toward the garden, elbowing each other out of the way.

The girls could see the top of the tent
from their hiding place in the tree.

"It looks like it's made of icing," said
Kirsty.

Nina nodded sadly. "It's fondant
icing," she said. "Jack Frost has taken all
the best sweet treats! Come on, let's
follow the goblins to the tent. If that's
where Jack Frost is, then that's where my
charm and Kirsty's cake are, too!"

The three friends fluttered into the air
and raced after the goblins. They flew
high above the milkshake moat so they
wouldn't be seen. The goblins looked like
tiny green specks below! As they
disappeared into the tent, the fairies
hovered side by side and looked at one
another.

"We have to go inside," said Rachel.

The others nodded, looking nervous. They didn't know what they'd find in there. They waited until the last goblin had entered the tent. Then they held hands and swooped down through the entrance.

The space inside the tent was packed with goblins. At one end was a round stage that looked like frosted tiers of cake. Jack Frost was sitting on the top tier on a candy-cane throne! His hands rested on the arms of the chair, and he glared at the crowd of goblins. At the other end of the tent was a huge blue box with a silver bow on top.

"Look," said Nina in a whisper.

"Kirsty's birthday cake is on the table in front of Jack Frost!"

"And your magic birthday candle charm is on that chain around his wrist," added Kirsty with a gasp.

"But look at all the goblins in here," said Rachel. "How are we ever going to get the charm back without being spotted?"

Just then, the town-crier goblin climbed onto the lowest tier of the cake stage and rang his bell. Nina, Kirsty, and Rachel hid behind a large bunch of balloons made of bubble-gum bubbles. They were close to the long-nosed goblin who had been nibbling on the chocolate tree.

"Listen!" the town crier squawked. "All goblins will now sing 'Happy Birthday,' led by everyone's favorite musicians."

He pointed to the big blue box at the far end of the tent. With an explosion of silver glitter, Frosty's Gobolicious Band burst out of the box and started to sing!

Fairies Under Attack!

As all the goblins joined in, the girls covered their ears. Every goblin seemed to be singing a different song to a different tune! Rachel couldn't help but giggle when she heard the words that the long-nosed goblin was singing:

"Happy birthday to you,
Mashed potatoes and stew!
You look like an elephant,
And you smell like one, too!"

Luckily, Jack Frost didn't hear him. He was too busy blowing out the candles on the cake. Once he did, there was a stampede! All the goblins wanted a piece of birthday cake. They bolted up the steps of the stage, until Jack Frost sprang to his feet with a yell.

"STOP!" he bellowed.

The goblins froze. Some of them had started to drool. Their master's eyes were blazing with rage.

"No one is having any birthday cake until I get some PRESENTS!" Jack Frost shouted.

The goblins looked down and shuffled their feet.

"The thing is . . ."

"It was such short notice . . ."

"We didn't have much time . . ."

"NOT GOOD ENOUGH!" roared Jack Frost.

In desperation, the
town-crier goblin
leaned forward
and puckered
his lips.

"Would
you like me
to give you a
birthday kiss?"
"Ugh!"
hollered Jack Frost.

He shoved the goblin backward, who
fell on top of three other goblins. Nina,
Rachel, and Kirsty put their hands over
their mouths to stifle their giggles.

"You can give me my presents later,"
announced Jack Frost. "Band, play 'For
He's a Jolly Good Fellow'—NOW!"

The band began to play, and the

goblins made a halfhearted attempt to
sing along. But they were impatient!
They wanted birthday cake, and some of
them couldn't wait any longer. The girls
saw them start to lick the candy-cane
throne.

"Stop that, you greedy fools!" Jack
Frost demanded. "Fine, come and get
some cake."

"Oh, no!" exclaimed Nina.

Jack Frost cut the
thinnest slivers of
cake that he could
and handed them
out to the goblins.
Then he picked up
a big chunk of cake
and opened his mouth wide. The magic
charm glimmered on his wrist. Seeing it

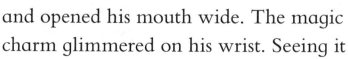

again was too much for Nina.

"I want my charm back!" she cried.

She darted out from behind the balloons and zoomed toward Jack Frost. Rachel and Kirsty flew close behind. Everyone was so busy eating cake that they didn't see the three fairies coming! Nina zipped down next to Jack Frost's hand and started to undo the chain that held the charm. Rachel and Kirsty held their breath in excitement, fluttering above in case Nina needed their help. Could she get the charm back without anyone noticing?

Just then, Jack Frost tilted his head back to take another bite of cake and saw Rachel and Kirsty hovering above his head.

"Fairies!" he snarled, raising his wand. "We're infested with fairies!"

He sent a bolt of icy magic crackling toward them. Rachel and Kirsty were hurled sideways.

"Stop that!" cried Nina. "Leave them alone!"

She grabbed his wand, trying to yank it out of his hands. Jack Frost gave a mean laugh and flicked the wand, sending Nina tumbling across the tent.

"You'll never get your charm back!" he shouted.

Rachel and Kirsty caught Nina, who shook her head dizzily.

"Look out!" cried Kirsty.

They dodged another bolt of magic, which hit the bubble-gum balloons behind them. There was a huge *bang* and all the balloons burst, covering the goblins in a sticky mess.

"My outfit!" squealed the town crier.

The other goblins tried to pull his costume off, but they just got stuck together. Every time they touched anything, they stuck to it! While the

goblins all squawked and wailed, Jack
Frost grabbed the rest of the cake and
dashed out of the tent.

"Follow him!" cried Rachel. "We can't
let him out of our sight!"

Jack Frost Takes a Dip

The fairies flew after Jack Frost as he ran, cackling, into the Candy Castle. He stumbled over broken cobblestones made of gobstoppers, then raced up a winding sugar staircase to the top of the tallest tower. The fairies were close behind him, but as soon as they flew out of the stairwell, Jack Frost flung a series of hailstones at them, stinging their faces and hands.

The fairies ducked behind the railing
and tried to catch
their breath.

"You'll never stop
me now." Jack Frost
gloated through a
mouthful of birthday
cake. "Your charm is
mine forever!"

He jingled the charm that was still
dangling around his wrist, and shoved
another piece of cake into his mouth.

"What are we going to do?" asked
Nina. "As long as he has his wand, we
can't get close to him!"

"Maybe we don't need to," said Kirsty
thoughtfully. "Remember how angry he
got when the goblins licked his candy-
cane throne? Maybe if we eat some of

his castle, he'll forget to be so careful
with the charm."

They all flew down the side of the
tower and hovered below the railing,
close to a small window. The window
frame was made of fudge. Kirsty winked
at Rachel and Nina.

"Mmm!" she said in a loud voice.
"These window frames are delicious!"

"Scrumptious!" added Rachel at the
top of her voice. "Maybe we should just
forget about the charm and eat the
Candy Castle, instead."

"STOP THAT!" Jack
Frost roared, leaning
over the railing and
shaking his fist.

The fairies looked up
and rubbed their tummies.

"I've never tasted such wonderful fudge," said Nina, licking her lips.

"Leave that window frame alone!" Jack Frost shrieked. "It's MINE!"

"We'll leave right now if you give back Nina's charm," said Kirsty.

"NO DEAL!" Jack Frost snarled.

He sent magic bolts raining down on them, but the fairies just pressed themselves against the wall and laughed.

"You can't stop us from eating," called Rachel, pretending to pick off a piece of windowsill. "You can't even reach us from up there."

"Oh, I CAN'T?" Jack Frost replied in a fury.

With that, he leaned so far over the edge that he almost fell off! As he pointed his wand downward, trying to aim at the fairies, the charm slipped off his wrist—and he dropped his wand!

"NOOO!" Jack Frost wailed as the chain and magic charm plummeted down.

"Catch the charm!" cried Nina.

Rachel zoomed over, but she was half a second too late. The charm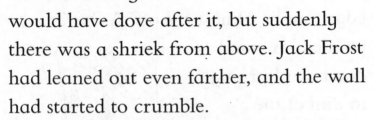
was still falling! She would have dove after it, but suddenly there was a shriek from above. Jack Frost had leaned out even farther, and the wall had started to crumble.

"The wall is weak because of the goblins' snacking," said Kirsty with a gasp. "It's full of holes!"

Before Nina could raise her wand to help, the wall collapsed. Jack Frost hurtled down, the birthday cake close behind!

"HELP!" he wailed.

Before the fairies could do anything, he disappeared into the moat with a gigantic *splash*! Frothy milkshake flew into the air and covered the banks of the moat. The fairies zoomed down and saw Jack Frost bob to the surface. He spit out a mouthful of milkshake and splashed wildly.

"Help!" he shouted again. "Come here, you useless goblins! Get me out of here!"

But all his goblins were still stuck together with bubble gum in the tent. Kirsty pointed to something lying on the bank.

"There's a branch of the chocolate tree that's been nibbled off!" she exclaimed. "We could use it to pull him out."

Together, the three fairies flew over the middle of the moat and held the branch out to Jack Frost.

"Grab the end of this, and we'll pull you to the shore," Rachel said.

Jack Frost clutched at the branch, and the fairies hauled him to the bank of the moat. As he lay there, gasping and soggy, the three friends looked at one another.

"Jack Frost is safe," said Kirsty. "But where is Nina's magic charm?"

"It must have sunk in the moat," said Nina, holding back tears. "Oh, girls, it's gone forever!"

The girls held Nina's hands, feeling terrible. Then, out of the corner of her eye, Rachel saw something glimmering on the surface of the moat.

"Maybe not!" she said, darting out above the moat again.

The milkshake bubbles were making
the little birthday candle charm dance
on the surface. It almost looked like the
moat was playing with it! Rachel
reached the charm and scooped it up.
Then she flew back to the bank and
handed it to Nina. The charm
immediately shrank to fairy-size, and
Nina's eyes welled up
with happy tears
as she slipped it
onto her wrist.

"I can't believe
it!" she said. "All
seven of the Sugar
and Spice Fairies'
charms are finally back
where they belong!"

"Yes — and look what's happening to the Candy Castle," said Kirsty.

As they watched, Jack Frost's new castle seemed to melt away. Jack Frost leaped to his feet and jumped up and down in a rage. On the other side of the moat, he could see the sticky goblins crawling out of the tent, gobbling up the last traces of treats.

"Stop that!" he hollered. "Those are mine, do you hear me? MINE!"

"Hasn't this taught you a lesson?" Rachel asked him. "You shouldn't be so greedy!"

He just shook his fist at her.

"I think it's time for us to leave," said Nina with a laugh.

She waved her wand, and in a twinkling of fairy dust, the girls were standing in the Fairyland Candy Factory. The last time they had been here, it had been a very sad place. Because Jack Frost had stolen the Sugar and Spice Fairies' charms, the candies and treats had all been ruined.

"What a difference!" said Kirsty, looking around in relief.

Now the trees were heavy with yummy goodies. They looked wonderful! Fat scoops of lemon sherbet, orange ice cream, and strawberry sorbet hung from the branches. The six other Sugar and Spice Fairies were already there, filling

the Treat Day baskets. When they saw
the girls and Nina, they sped over and
gathered them in a big fairy hug, their
wings fluttering together.

"You did it!" cheered Madeline the
Cookie Fairy. "When the orchard came
back to life, we knew you must have
been helping Nina. Thank you!"

"Yes," said a beautiful voice behind them. "We thank you from the bottom of our hearts."

The fairies turned and saw Queen Titania and King Oberon smiling at them. Honey the Candy Fairy was at their side, and their arms were filled with baskets of chewy cookies, gooey chocolates, and beautiful cupcakes.

"We're here to finish the Treat Day baskets," Queen Titania went on. "We're so grateful for your help, Kirsty and Rachel. Treat Day would not be happening without you! Once again, you've shown us that you are Fairyland's best friends."

"There's a big slice of birthday cake going into each fairy's basket in honor of your birthday, Kirsty," added Honey.

"Thank you for everything," said Nina, giving them a final hug. "But now it's time for you to go back to the human world. There's a party waiting for you!"

She winked and
raised her wand.
A flurry of
rainbow-
colored fairy
dust swirled
around the
girls and
lifted them
into the air.

When the sparkles
faded, they were back in Kirsty's kitchen.
The music was still playing in the next
room, and they heard the doorbell
ringing.

"No time has passed at all," said
Rachel in awe, looking up at the clock.
"That's one of the most wonderful things
about Fairyland."

"Yes," said Kirsty, smiling at her best friend, "and it means that my birthday lasts even longer!"

Just then, Aunt Helen came hurrying into the kitchen with another box from Cupcake Corner.

"This was just delivered," she said, sounding excited. "Look, girls! They must have heard that something happened to the other cake. This one's even prettier!"

She lifted the lid of the box, and
Rachel and Kirsty peered inside. They
saw another rose-colored birthday cake
that said HAPPY BIRTHDAY, KIRSTY on it,
just like the one that Jack Frost had
stolen. But this one had seven little fairies
on top made of fondant . . . seven little
fairies who looked very familiar! Kirsty
and Rachel shared a secret smile. The
fairies on the cake looked just like the
Sugar and Spice Fairies!

Aunt Helen put the cake on a plate and lit the candles. Then she dimmed the lights, and all of Kirsty's friends and family came into the kitchen to sing "Happy Birthday." Kirsty closed her eyes, made a special birthday wish, and blew out the candles.

As everyone cheered and the lights went on, Rachel squeezed Kirsty's hand. "What did you wish for?" she asked.

"I can't tell you that, or it won't happen," said Kirsty with a laugh. "And this is a wish I really want to come true!"

But Rachel could guess what her best
friend had wished for. They both wanted
more magical fun with their fairy
friends. Hopefully, another adventure
was just around the corner!

THE EARTH FAIRIES

Rachel and Kirsty found the
Sugar and Spice Fairies' missing
magic charms. Now it's time for them
to help the Earth Fairies!

Join their next adventure in
this special sneak peek of

Nicole
the Beach Fairy!

Time for Action

"Isn't it wonderful to be back on Rainspell Island again, Rachel?" Kirsty Tate said happily, gazing out over the shimmering blue-green sea. "It hasn't changed a bit!"

Rachel Walker, Kirsty's best friend, nodded. "Rainspell is still as beautiful as ever," she replied as the two girls followed the rocky path down to the beach. "This is one of the most special places in the whole world!"

The Tates and the Walkers were spending school break on Rainspell Island. Even though it was fall, the sky was a clear blue and the sun was shining brightly, so it felt more like summer. Kirsty and Rachel couldn't wait to get to the beach and dip their toes in the ocean.

"You're right, Rachel," Kirsty agreed, her eyes twinkling. "After all, this is where we first became friends!"

"And we found lots of other amazing friends here, too, didn't we?" Rachel laughed.

"This is gorgeous!" Kirsty said as they finally reached the beach.

The golden sand seemed to stretch for miles into the distance. Seagulls soared in the sky, and Kirsty could smell the fresh, salty sea air. "Should we explore the rock pools?" she suggested.

But Rachel didn't reply. She was looking down the beach, her face clouded with dismay.

"Haven't you noticed the litter, Kirsty?" she asked, pointing ahead of them.

Kirsty stared at the golden sand more closely. To her horror, down near the water's edge, she could see some plastic bags blowing around in the breeze. There were also some soda cans and empty water bottles floating in the ocean.

"Oh, Rachel, this is awful!" Kirsty exclaimed. "I don't remember seeing *any* litter last time we were here."

Kirsty shaded her eyes and looked farther down the beach. She could see even more litter strewn across the sand.

"Rachel, we have to do something about this." Kirsty had a determined look on her face. "Rainspell Island is beautiful, and we have to keep it that way. We'll need help, though—and I know just where we can get it!"

Rachel's face lit up. "Fairyland!" she burst out excitedly.

RAINBOW magic™

Which Magical Fairies Have You Met?

- ☐ The Rainbow Fairies
- ☐ The Weather Fairies
- ☐ The Jewel Fairies
- ☐ The Pet Fairies
- ☐ The Dance Fairies
- ☐ The Music Fairies
- ☐ The Sports Fairies
- ☐ The Party Fairies
- ☐ The Ocean Fairies
- ☐ The Night Fairies
- ☐ The Magical Animal Fairies
- ☐ The Princess Fairies
- ☐ The Superstar Fairies
- ☐ The Fashion Fairies
- ☐ The Sugar & Spice Fairies

■ SCHOLASTIC

Find all of your favorite fairy friends at
scholastic.com/rainbowmagic

HiT entertainment

RMFAIRY9

RAINBOW *magic*™ **SPECIAL EDITION**

Which Magical Fairies Have You Met?

3 stories in each one!

- ☐ Joy the Summer Vacation Fairy
- ☐ Holly the Christmas Fairy
- ☐ Kylie the Carnival Fairy
- ☐ Stella the Star Fairy
- ☐ Shannon the Ocean Fairy
- ☐ Trixie the Halloween Fairy
- ☐ Gabriella the Snow Kingdom Fairy
- ☐ Juliet the Valentine Fairy
- ☐ Mia the Bridesmaid Fairy
- ☐ Flora the Dress-Up Fairy
- ☐ Paige the Christmas Play Fairy
- ☐ Emma the Easter Fairy
- ☐ Cara the Camp Fairy
- ☐ Destiny the Rock Star Fairy
- ☐ Belle the Birthday Fairy
- ☐ Olympia the Games Fairy
- ☐ Selena the Sleepover Fairy
- ☐ Cheryl the Christmas Tree Fairy
- ☐ Florence the Friendship Fairy
- ☐ Lindsay the Luck Fairy
- ☐ Brianna the Tooth Fairy
- ☐ Autumn the Falling Leaves Fairy
- ☐ Keira the Movie Star Fairy
- ☐ Addison the April Fool's Day Fairy

■ SCHOLASTIC

Find all of your favorite fairy friends at
scholastic.com/rainbowmagic

HIT entertainment

RMSPECIAL12